How the Ladybug Got Her Spots

Written by Caren Green
Illustrated by Bethany Goossen

Once in the leafy, green plants lived a small red and black bug.

2

All of the creatures that lived in
the garden were very special in
their own unique ways.

The butterfly had very pretty, colorful wings.

The caterpillar had tickly, short fur.

And the spider had all eight of her wonderful legs.

 5

One day, the little red bug began to think
that she was not special.

She felt plain and ordinary,

so she decided to leave her home in
the leafy, green garden...

8

to search for something that
would make her as special as all of
her garden friends.

After hours of searching, it started to rain.

The little red bug landed to
take shelter under a nice tall piece
of grass. She was disappointed that
she had not found what she was
looking for, and did not know
where to explore next.

While she waited for the rain to stop, she thought of her friends in the garden: the butterfly with her pretty, colorful wings, the caterpillar with her tickly, short fur, the spider, with her eight wonderful legs.

She had not found anything that would make her any different, so she sadly decided to turn around and go home as she was.

14

But as she flew along, she passed
through...

a rainbow!

16

The wet colors of the rainbow mixed together on her wings.

Soon she had little black dots all over.

17

She smiled to think that she had
accidentally found a way to be
different after she had given up.

Her friends were as surprised as
she was when she got home.
"We were so worried about you!"
said the butterfly.
"Where did you get those spots?"
asked the caterpillar.

19

"I went away searching for something to make me special. I found these spots, but I feel just the same no matter how I look."

"You were always special," said the spider. "You were always you."